WUTHERING HEIGHTS

EMILY BRONTË

adapted by Shirley Isherwood

OXFORD
UNIVERSITY PRESS

OXFORD
UNIVERSITY PRESS

Great Clarendon Street, Oxford OX2 6DP

Oxford University Press is a department of the University of Oxford.
It furthers the University's objective of excellence in research, scholarship,
and education by publishing worldwide in

Oxford   New York
Auckland   Cape Town   Dar es Salaam   Hong Kong   Karachi
Kuala Lumpur   Madrid   Melbourne   Mexico City   Nairobi
New Delhi   Shanghai   Taipei   Toronto

With offices in

Argentina   Austria   Brazil   Chile   Czech Republic   France   Greece
Guatemala   Hungary   Italy   Japan   Poland   Portugal   Singapore
South Korea   Switzerland   Thailand   Turkey   Ukraine   Vietnam

Oxford is a registered trade mark of Oxford University Press
in the UK and in certain other countries

British Library Cataloguing in Publication Data
Data available

ISBN 13: 978-0-19-918480-4
ISBN 10: 0-19-918480-1

1 3 5 7 9 10 8 6 4 2

Cover: Stock Illustration Source/Michael Cacy
Inside illustrations: Zhenya Matysiak

Printed in Great Britain by Ashford Colour Press, Gosport, Hants

About the Author

EMILY BRONTË

1818–1848

Emily was the daughter of a vicar in Yorkshire, where she lived with her brother and her sisters, who also wrote books.

Emily was quiet, but fiery. When she wanted to stop the family bulldog sleeping on the beds, she fiercely beat his head with her fists. Even so, the dog did not stop loving her, and when Emily died, it slept in her empty room, moaning.

Wuthering Heights was published a year before Emily died. It was a success, although the cruelty of the characters upset many readers. It is still a very popular book and has been adapted for television, radio and film many times.

CHAPTER I

I visit Wuthering Heights

Late one afternoon, I rode over the moors to Wuthering Heights. It was not a good idea to have made this ride, for the weather turned cold, and it began to snow. When I reached the yard I found it empty, except for one old man, who poked his head out of a window of the barn.

'What do you want?' he asked, in a surly voice. 'Master's down in the fold, seeing to the animals.'

The snow by now was driving harder into my face, and coating my jacket and breeches in white. I shivered in every limb.

'Is there no one in the house who can let me in?' I asked.

'There's only the missis,' the old man answered, 'and you can knock until nightfall before *she'd* open the door to you.'

He withdrew his head. As I stood wondering what to do next, a tall handsome man came striding through the yard.

'Mr Heathcliff!' I cried. 'I'm Mr Lockwood, your new tenant of Thrushcross Grange. Perhaps this was not the best of times to pay you a visit . . . '

'There is no "perhaps" about it, Mr Lockwood,' he said. 'Only a fool would have left his house on such a day.'

Without giving me time to reply – though in truth, I was struck speechless by the rudeness of his remark – he turned and bellowed, 'Joseph!'

The face of the bad-tempered old man appeared once more at the window.

'Take Mr Lockwood's horse,' said Heathcliff, 'and bring us some wine.'

He strode in the direction of the house and I followed. Flinging open the door, he ushered me into the living room, and then left by another door.

What a room it was! A great fire burned at one end, the flames reflected in row upon row of silver dishes that stood on a huge oak dresser. In an arch under the dresser lay a pointer bitch with a litter of puppies.

Seated before the fire was a young woman scarcely older than a child, I thought, and with the prettiest face I had ever seen. A young man crouched on a low stool, close by. Neither spoke to me.

'A fine animal, madam,' I said, thinking to break the silence and pointing to the dog. 'Are you going to keep any of the young ones?'

'They are not mine,' the young woman answered shortly.

'Ah, your favourites are amongst these,' said I, pointing to a chair that held what I thought to be a cushion full of cats, but which turned out to be the bodies of dead rabbits.

'A strange choice,' she said, her voice cold and filled with scorn.

The young man sniggered. 'I shot them this morning,' he said. At this, I felt more foolish than ever, and held my tongue.

After staring at me for some seconds, the young woman rose and, standing on tiptoe, reached up to take hold of a canister which stood on the chimney shelf. 'Were you asked to tea?' she demanded.

'I should be glad of a cup,' I answered.

'Were you *asked*?' she repeated.

'Well, no,' I said. My words caused her to put the canister back in its place and to fling herself back into her chair.

Heathcliff came into the room at this moment, followed by Joseph, who carried a tray with wine-glasses.

'You must forgive us, Mr Lockwood,' he said. 'We get so few visitors at Wuthering Heights that we no longer know how to treat them.'

'My visit was not made at the best of times,' I murmured. 'I am new to this part of the country and did not know how bad the weather could turn, and so quickly.' I glanced towards the window as I spoke. Already the snow lay inches thick on the sills.

'Now I fear that I must put you to more trouble and ask that you lend me one of your lads to show me the way back. He could sleep at the Grange until morning.'

'I can't do that,' said Heathcliff. 'I need all my lads.'

'Then I must trust to my own judgement,' I said, 'and make my way as best I can.' I drank my wine in one gulp, and rose from my chair. I was angry at myself for making this untimely visit, and for suffering so meekly the rude manner in which I had been treated.

'Sit down, sir,' said Heathcliff. 'You shall stay the night as my guest.' The tone of his voice was anything but welcoming, but there was little I could do except sit down again, as he suggested.

A meal was brought to the table by a stout, red-cheeked smiling servant. She at least raised my spirits a little, and it was she, who, when the meal was ended, showed me to the room which was to be mine for the night.

'Here, sir,' she said, flinging open a door, 'Mr Heathcliff says you are to sleep in here.'

What a smell of decay met our nostrils! The servant, Zillah, glanced at me, and took a step inside. The light of her candle showed us nothing but a bed and a pine chest and some rotting curtains that hung at the windows.

'Come, sir,' she whispered, and led me across the landing to another chamber. This was a much better room. I noticed that it had a curious window seat, which could be closed by a pair of shutters like doors, thus hiding the occupant from anyone who entered.

I thanked Zillah, and promised that I would be as quiet as I could. Then, finding that the window seat was more comfortable than the bed, I placed my candle on the little shelf inside and stretched myself full length upon the bench.

As I did so, my eye was caught by the name 'Catherine' scratched over and over again in the paint. 'Catherine Earnshaw,' I read, 'Catherine Linton. Catherine Heathcliff.' Who was she? I wondered, drowsily.

But tired though I was, the howling of the wind outside made it impossible to sleep. Seeing a pile of old books stacked in a corner of the shelf I took one up and opened it. It had been used, I found, as a kind of diary. The blank end-pages and some of the margins were covered in writing. 'Catherine Earnshaw – her book' was the title given in a childish scrawl.

'An awful Sunday!' read one entry. 'I wish that Father were here. Hindley has acted with such cruelty! Heathcliff and I are going to revolt!'

'All day it has rained hard,' read another entry. 'We could not go to church, so Joseph took it upon himself to preach to us – which he did for two long boring hours.'

The third entry of the diary read, 'How little did I dream that

Hindley could make me cry so! Poor Heathcliff! Hindley says that he's a vagabond and won't let him sit with us, or eat with us any more. He says that I mustn't play with him, and threatens to turn him out of the house if I do.'

I wondered for a while who was the Catherine who had written the diary, and who was Hindley – and what had they to do with Joseph and Heathcliff; then the wind died down for a time and ceased its wailing, and at last I fell asleep.

I did not sleep long. I was awakened by the sound of something tapping at the windowpane. Peering though the glass I saw that the snow was still falling, the flakes whirling in the wind. As I tried to see further, the tapping came again, more loudly and more urgently than ever. 'It's the branch of a tree,' I told myself, 'and I must try to remove it, else there'll be no further rest for me tonight.'

I tried to open the window. The glass broke and I reached through it. To my horror, my fingers were grasped by a little ice-cold hand. I tried to withdraw my arm, but the cold fingers clung to me and a voice sobbed, 'Let me in . . . let me in!'

'Who are you?' I asked, now so frozen with terror that I no longer tried to move.

'Catherine Linton,' replied the voice. 'I lost my way on the moor. I'm come home . . . ' As the voice spoke I thought I saw the face of a girl at the window. 'It's twenty years,' she sobbed, 'I've been a waif for twenty years!'

'Be gone!' I shouted. 'Whatever you are, spirit, demon, ghost . . . !'

My cry was answered by Heathcliff, who flung open the chamber door.

'Who put you in here?' he demanded. 'I've a good mind to turn them out of the house!'

'Your servant, Zillah,' I said, 'and I shouldn't care if you did turn her out. I suppose that she wanted to get proof that the place is haunted. You may tell her from me that it is!'

'Lie down and finish your sleep,' said Heathcliff, 'and don't repeat that horrid yell. Nothing could excuse it, unless you were having your throat cut.'

'If that little fiend had got in at the window, she would probably have strangled me,' I returned.

For a moment, he was silent, then, 'Get out,' he said. His voice was quieter, but its tone frightened me.

'Gladly,' I replied. 'I won't stay another moment in this house. I'll walk about the yard until day.'

'Do as you please,' he said shortly, closing the door on me. I paused for a moment on the landing, and heard him speak, his voice this time filled with sorrow.

'Come in, come in! Cathy, do come! My heart's darling, hear me *this* time . . . '

I made my way to the living room where the remains of the fire still glowed under a covering of white ash.

At first light, I went into the yard and down to the gate, and was about to strike out across the moor, when I was stopped by a call from the door of the house.

It was the young man whom I had met in the afternoon. He told me that his name was Hareton Earnshaw, and that he would show me the way to Thrushcross Grange.

It was as well that he did, for the entire countryside was now one mass of white billowing snow. We spoke little during our journey, although there was much I longed to ask him. He left me at the gates of the Grange, and I staggered up the drive, and went to my study, feeling as weak as a kitten.

CHAPTER 2

Nelly Begins her Story

The next day I woke up with a bad cold. I also felt lonely. All day I longed for company, and when my servant, Nelly Dean, brought in my supper tray I asked her to stay.

'Tell me about Heathcliff,' I said, curious to learn more about this strange man, and indeed about all the inhabitants of Wuthering Heights. (Of the spirit at the window I did not speak, fearing that she might think me mad.) 'Do you know anything about him?'

'Know anything of him, sir?' said Nelly. 'Why, I was there when he was first brought to the house!'

◆◆◆

I was often at Wuthering Heights in those days, helping with the hay and at whatever task they gave me. One day, it came about that my master, Mr Earnshaw, went on a journey to Liverpool. He returned carrying his great coat bundled in his arms, and tired beyond words, but smiling.

'See, wife,' he said, 'I was never so beaten with anything in my life, but you must take it as a gift from God, although it's as dark as if it came from the devil.'

What tumbled out from the coat was a dirty ragged child. It was old enough to walk and talk but it did neither; instead it glared all around itself, uttering some gibberish that none of us understood. Heaven keep *me*, I thought, from ever receiving such a gift, either from the Almighty or from Lucifer!

Mrs Earnshaw was all for throwing it out of the house. 'How could you bring a gypsy brat like this to our home,' she demanded, 'when we have our own children to feed and clothe? What do you mean to do with it? Are you mad?'

Oh, she ranted on, sir, and I felt that none could blame her. The master, half-dead from fatigue, tried to explain what had happened, but all that I could make out between the mistress' scoldings was the fact that he had found the child homeless and all but starving in the streets of Liverpool. No one could tell him to whom the child belonged, and he was determined not to leave it to die in the gutter.

'Wash it and give it clean clothes,' my master told me, 'and let it sleep with the children.' That was Miss Cathy and Master Hindley, sir, his son and daughter.

Well, I bathed it, as asked, and then put it on the stair landing, from where I secretly hoped it might creep away in the night.

It didn't creep away, sir, but crept instead to Mr Earnshaw's bedroom door, where he found it in the morning.

I was sent away from the house, as a punishment for my cold heart. When I returned I found that the child had been christened Heathcliff, and that he and Miss Cathy had become great friends already. The two would be about the same age, six or seven years old.

Hindley was fourteen, and he hated Heathcliff. As for the mistress, she never put in a good word for him when she saw him wronged. And he was wronged a good deal. This made old Mr Earnshaw sad, as he had taken to the boy in a way that he had never taken to his own son, or indeed to Miss Cathy.

Oh, Master Hindley was a whiner, sir, forever complaining if he didn't get his own way. As for

Miss Cathy, she was far too mischievous to be a favourite.

But Heathcliff, although he was a patient, silent, hardworking child, was far from perfect. I'll give you an instance.

One day the master bought two colts at a fair and gave one to each of the lads. Heathcliff chose the most handsome of the two, but it soon went lame.

'You must exchange horses with me,' he told Hindley. 'If you don't I shall tell your father about the three beatings you've given me this week.'

'Get away, dog!' cried Hindley, seeing Heathcliff's movement towards his pony. He bent and lifted an iron weight used for weighing potatoes, and threatened to throw it.

'Throw it,' said Heathcliff, not moving an inch, 'and I'll tell how you boast that you'll turn me out of the house when he dies. See if he won't throw *you* out instead.'

Hindley threw the weight, catching the child in the chest. Down he fell, but staggered up at once, breathless and white.

'Take my colt then, gypsy!' said young Earnshaw, 'and I pray he may break your neck!'

Heathcliff had already started to move the animal to his own stable, even as Hindley spoke. Enraged by this, Hindley knocked him under the pony's feet. But

Heathcliff coolly gathered himself up, and without a word began to exchange the saddles.

So from the very beginning Heathcliff bred bad feeling. Hindley saw him as someone who had stolen his father's love and his rights as the son of the house. Whenever he got the chance he bullied and beat the child. Heathcliff never told tales, but he always let Hindley know that he would do so if and when it suited him.

At last, not knowing what else to do, Mr Earnshaw sent Hindley away to college.

Now, I thought, we will have some peace – and so we might have done had it not been for Miss Cathy and Joseph. Joseph was, and is, the most wearisome old man, quoting the Bible at every turn, seeing sins and faults in others and telling a long string of tales about Cathy and Heathcliff.

Certainly Miss Cathy had ways with her that I never before saw in a child. And she could make us lose patience fifty times a day. Her spirits were always high, and she was forever laughing, singing, talking – and she was much too fond of Heathcliff. The greatest punishment we could give her was to separate her from him.

Then, one day – with Cathy for once sitting quietly by his side, and Heathcliff at his feet – old Mr Earnshaw died.

When Cathy realized that her father was gone from her, she sobbed so piteously that none who heard her could have doubted for a moment how dearly she had loved him.

Hindley came home at once, and surprised us all by bringing a wife with him. She was a nice young thing, but thin, sir, and I noticed she coughed a lot.

The first thing that Hindley did on his return was to tell me and Joseph that in future we were to live in the kitchen, leaving the house to himself and his wife.

As for Heathcliff, he was no longer to have lessons with Cathy, and was sent to work outside with the farmhands. He didn't mind this too much at first. Cathy taught him all she learned and worked and played with him in the fields.

Oh, they were like a pair of savages, and what they loved most was to run away to the moors and stay there all day. They hid themselves away so often that one evening, when they didn't return for supper, Master Hindley locked the doors and told us that we were not to let them in.

But I was too worried to sleep. I sat by my bedroom window, gazing out, and after a while I saw a light glimmering down by the gate. I threw a shawl over my head and ran down and found Heathcliff. He was alone.

'Where's Miss Cathy?' I cried.

'At Thrushcross Grange,' he replied.

'Catherine was *here*!' I cried. After reading snatches of her diary and hearing Nelly speak so vividly of her she had become a live, breathing being to me. Indeed, I half-expected the door to open and for her to stand there.

'Oh, indeed yes,' said Nelly. 'Catherine was here. In time, Catherine became the mistress of Thrushcross Grange.

'But it's late, sir,' she added. 'The story will keep until tomorrow.' Gathering up my tray and her knitting, at which she had worked while she told her tale, she left the room.

CHAPTER 3

Cathy at Thrushcross Grange

The next evening I could hardly wait for Nelly to arrive with my tray and her knitting. But at last the hour came.

'Catherine was here, at Thrushcross,' I reminded her. But my storyteller needed no prompting.

'Indeed she was, sir,' said Nelly, 'and Heathcliff stood shivering at the gate, his clothes wet through. "They had not the manners to ask *me*," he said.'

I hurried him into the kitchen, by way of the wash house, and after he had changed his clothes, he told me what had happened.

'Cathy and I had been on the moors all day,' he said. 'When night fell we saw the lights come on in Thrushcross Grange.

' "Let's go and see if the little Lintons spend *their* Sunday evenings shivering in corners," I said, "while their elders eat and drink in comfort!" '

(Linton was the name of the family who owned Thrushcross Grange in those days.)

'We ran from the top of the Heights to the grounds of

the house. I beat Cathy in the race. Then we crept through a broken hedge, and climbed up on to the big flowerpots that stood beneath the window. Oh, Nelly, what a beautiful place it is! All crimson carpet and sparkling lights. The little Lintons, Edgar and his sister, had the room to themselves. Don't you think they ought to have been happy? We would have thought ourselves in heaven! But Isabella, who is eleven, a year younger than Cathy, was lying on the hearthrug, shrieking, and Edgar stood weeping close by. In the middle of all this, sat a little dog, the cause of the upset. Each had wanted to hold it, and now neither held it. Oh, we laughed aloud, Cathy and I, at the sight.

'The Lintons heard us, looked up and saw our faces at the window. They shrieked in earnest then, and their parents rushed into the room. I pulled Cathy down from her perch and we ran back over the gardens. But suddenly, she fell.

' "Run, Heathcliff! Run!" she whispered. "They have let the bulldog loose and he's got me."

'The devil dog had seized her by her ankle! I took up a big stone and tried to thrust it between his teeth, but the creature held on until the servants came running and took him by the collar. The man then lifted Cathy and carried her to the house. I followed.

' "What have you got there, Robert?" called Mr Linton from the steps.

'"Skulker's caught a little girl, sir, Mr Earnshaw's daughter," answered Robert, "and there's a lad here too, a regular gypsy by the look of him."

'"Why, it's that half-savage creature that Earnshaw brought back from Liverpool! Be off with you!" cried Linton, as Cathy was carried into the house, and the door was slammed in my face. But I didn't leave, not I! I went back to the window and watched as Cathy was laid on the sofa and her ankle bathed and bandaged.

'Then they wheeled her chair to the fire, and gave her a glass of wine to sip. Isabella emptied a plate of little cakes into her lap, while that baby, Edgar, stood close by, speechless with admiration – and so he ought to be, for isn't she far better than anyone else on this earth, Nelly?

'I stayed for a while, until I was sure that she was settled and happy – for had she not been, I would have smashed the window to have got her away.

'But she did seem happy, and so I left and came back here.'

He threw himself down on the settle, and looking at him I thought, 'Yes, you would do anything for Cathy. She is your life, and you are hers.' Aloud, I said, 'There'll be trouble about this when Master Hindley finds out.'

And there was trouble, sir, but not in the way that I had expected. Hindley, when he learned of what had happened, forbade Heathcliff to even speak to Cathy when she returned. But Cathy stayed at Thrushcross Grange for five weeks. When she came back we scarcely recognized her. Gone was the wild tangled hair and the bare feet. In their place were glossy ringlets, shoes, and a way of speaking and acting towards us all so different that we stood in silent amazement at the change.

But her loving heart was not changed, sir. She would have thrown her arms round me, covered in flour as I was – for it was near Christmas and I was making the cake – had not Hindley checked her.

'Why, Cathy, what a little lady you have become,' he cried. 'What a beauty!' And saying this he and his wife, Frances, led her to the fire, and fussed over her in a way I never thought she would accept. But accept it she did; I never saw anyone so altered, and my thoughts flew to Heathcliff. How will he take this change, I wondered.

Since Cathy's absence he had gone from bad to worse. For days at a time he had simply come in from his work in the fields, eaten what was set before him, and either slept, or lay by the kitchen fire, gazing into the flames. And I had neither the time nor the inclination to bully him into washing, or to offer to wash his clothes. This was a fault on my part, sir, and one that I now bitterly regret. It put Heathcliff entirely at the mercy of Hindley, and Hindley of course had no mercy to show to his old enemy.

'Heathcliff, come!' he cried. 'You may wish Miss Cathy welcome, like the other servants.'

Heathcliff slowly entered the room, and at once Cathy jumped up, ran to him and threw her arms round his neck, laughing with delight and kissing his cheek over and over again. I saw Master Hindley and the mistress exchange satisfied glances.

'Oh, you have planned that this should happen!' I said to myself. 'Keeping him out in the fields till the last minute so that he looks rough and dirty beside the others – a mean trick!'

In the next moment, Cathy drew back and stared at her friend.

'Why, how dirty you are!' she exclaimed.

Heathcliff thrust her away from him. 'You needn't have touched me,' he said angrily, and dashed from the room.

I returned to the kitchen and my baking, for the master and mistress were to have visitors that night. But once everyone was sitting at ease with mulled wine before them, and all the gossip of the day to talk over, I ran out into the yard to look for Heathcliff. I found him in the stable, grooming one of the ponies.

'Make haste, Heathcliff,' I said, 'wash yourself, and change your clothes. You and Miss Cathy have the chance of the kitchen all to yourselves for an hour.'

He didn't turn his head or answer me, but went on brushing the pony.

'Come,' I said, 'I've made some little cakes for the two of you, and you can sit by the fire and chatter together to your heart's content, just as in the old days.'

Still I got no answer, and after waiting a moment longer I went back to the house.

But the next morning, he came to find me in the kitchen.

'Nelly,' he said, 'make me look decent. I think that Cathy no longer loves me but prefers Edgar Linton.'

Now was my chance, thought I, to undo a little of my unfeeling neglect, for the Lintons were to visit that day.

'Edgar Linton!' I said. 'Edgar Linton will look like a doll beside you by the time I've finished! You're younger and yet I swear you're taller, and broader in the shoulder than he.'

And so I rattled on, and in time made him clean and handsome. I even had him change into clean clothes, some of which I borrowed from my own young brother.

I had just completed this transformation when we heard the sound of wheels outside. Hurrying to the door, I saw Isabella and Edgar stepping out of the family carriage. Hindley and Frances rode by their side, and they dismounted from their horses. Catherine came running from the house, and taking the hands of the two children, led them inside.

I went back to the kitchen. 'Go now, and show yourself by the side of Edgar Linton, so that Cathy may see for herself who is the better,' I told Heathcliff.

He did as I bade him, but as luck would have it, when he opened the door to the living room he found Hindley standing on the other side. Hindley at once thrust him back.

Now, sir, I had made a meal for our visitors, and it lay spread on the table, a roast goose, tarts, fruits and hot savoury sauces.

'He'll be sticking his filthy fingers into the food,' said Hindley, seeing my expression.

'Yes, he does look something of a savage,' piped in Edgar Linton, who had peeped at Heathcliff from his seat by the fire. This remark brought a giggle from Isabella, and encouraged him to try further; for he had not received the response he had hoped for from Cathy.

'And just look at the colt's mane of hair hanging over his eyes,' he cried. 'It's a wonder it doesn't make his head ache!'

Straight away, Heathcliff darted back into the room, snatched up a dish of hot sauce and flung it into Edgar Linton's face.

Hindley seized him and dragged him from the room, and I've no doubt, gave him a good beating. Meanwhile

I had hurried to Edgar Linton's side, to wipe his face with a cloth. But Cathy turned on Linton. I saw the cold fury in her eyes, and contempt too, sir. Oh, she blazed with it!

'Why did you speak to him like that?' she demanded. 'Now he'll be whipped. I can't bear him to be whipped.'

'I didn't speak to him,' sobbed Edgar Linton, pushing me aside and finishing the job with his own handkerchief. 'I promised Mamma that I wouldn't, and I didn't.'

Hindley came back at this point, grinning and rubbing his hands.

'The next time, Linton,' he said, 'take the law into your own fists – it will give you an appetite for dinner!'

They sat at the table; Cathy ate little, but no one seemed to notice save I. In the evening the carol singers came, and later the band from Gimmerton, together with several guests from the village – oh, we were quite a party, sir.

Cathy loved it too, but said that she thought the music sounded sweetest from the head of the stairs. I followed her up to the top, but she did not stop there. Instead she climbed the steps to the garret where Heathcliff had been imprisoned by Hindley. Feeling sorry for them, I left them to talk with the garret door between them.

But when I returned, to warn Miss Cathy that the dancing and the music were coming to an end, imagine

my astonishment to find that their two voices came from
behind the door.

'How had this come about?' I asked Nelly, feeling astonishment
myself at this turn that the story had taken.

'Why, sir,' she told me, gathering up her workbasket and my
tray, 'the little monkey had crept out of the skylight of one attic,
and into the skylight of the attic where Heathcliff lay!' With that,
she prepared to take her leave.

CHAPTER 4

Cathy's Choice

'Nelly,' I said, 'do not stir from this room until you have told me
more of the story!'

'Very well, sir,' said Nelly, and took up her knitting again. 'But
I must make a leap of three years in my tale.'

'You will do nothing of the kind,' I told her.

'As you wish,' said Nelly. 'Then I will just pass to the next
summer, when Frances Earnshaw's baby was born.'

We were busy with the hay, when one of the girls came
running over the meadow, calling to us as she ran.

'Oh, such a grand baby!' she cried. 'The finest lad that ever breathed! But the mistress is dying. Doctor says she's had consumption for these many months, and will be dead before winter. You're to come back to the house at once, Nelly, for you are to look after the baby!'

I followed the girl, feeling a keen sorrow for Hindley. He adored his wife, and I couldn't think how he would bear the loss.

I found him standing by the door. 'Damn the doctor!' he told me. 'There's nothing wrong with Frances – nothing at all.' He almost persuaded me of the truth of this – certainly he convinced the mistress, for she seemed happy enough with her little son, but very weak. She remained like this for several weeks.

Then one night, as she leaned on his shoulder, saying that she thought that she might be able to get up for a little in the morning, she had a fit of coughing. It was only a slight one. He raised her in his arms, she put her two hands round his neck, and she was gone.

The child, Hareton, was now mine completely, to care for and love.

◆◆◆

'The young man at Wuthering Heights?' I interrupted. 'But surely, Nelly, since he is the son of Hindley Earnshaw, the house ought by rights to belong to him.'

'So it ought, sir,' said Nelly, 'but you will see how this did not come about.'

◆◆◆

After the death of his wife, Hindley fell into bad ways, drinking, gambling, and taking no interest in his son at all. He became a tyrant, and the servants at last would stand his behaviour no longer. They left, leaving just Joseph and me to care for everything.

The master's bad ways and bad companions were a poor example for Cathy and Heathcliff to follow. What an infernal house we had, sir. None would come near, unless you counted young Edgar Linton, who doted on Cathy. At fifteen she was the queen of the countryside, and as headstrong as ever. But he never came unless he was certain not to meet up with Hindley in one of his drunken rages.

Well, it came about that Hindley would be away from home for a day, and Heathcliff decided to give himself a holiday on the strength of this. He was sixteen by now, and a well-built, handsome lad. He strolled into the kitchen just as I was helping Cathy arrange her hair.

'Why are you wearing a silk dress?' he demanded.

'No reason,' said Cathy, her voice wavering, for she knew as well as I that Edgar Linton was due to pay a visit. 'Shouldn't you be in the fields by now?'

'Hindley doesn't often free us from his cursed presence,' replied Heathcliff. 'I'll work no more today, but stay with you.'

'But Joseph will tell!' said Cathy quickly, casting an anxious glance at me.

'Joseph is loading lime on the far side of Penistone Crags,' Heathcliff told her. 'He won't be back till dark.'

There was nothing for it but for Cathy to tell the truth. 'Isabella and Edgar Linton might call today,' she said.

'Get Nelly to tell them that you're out,' said Heathcliff, flinging himself down on the settle, frowning and surly. 'Look at the calendar there on the wall, Cathy. The crosses are for the evenings you've spent with the Lintons, the dots for the ones you've spent with me.'

Cathy lost her temper at these words, and stamped her foot. 'And should I always be sitting with you?' she demanded. 'What good do I get from that? What do you talk about? You might be dumb for all you say to amuse me, or for anything you do, come to that.'

Hindley had stopped Heathcliff's lessons with Cathy a long time ago, and he now seemed to have no desire to learn anything at all, even though I had heard Cathy say a hundred times that she would teach him all that she herself had been taught.

Heathcliff jumped up at her words, but there was no time for him to say anything about what he felt, for the sound of horses' hooves was heard outside. He rushed from the kitchen, as Edgar Linton came through the front door.

'I'm not too soon, am I?' he asked, casting a glance at me, for I had begun to dust the silver plates on the dresser, having had strict instructions from Hindley that the two of them must never be left alone.

Cathy came up behind me and whispered in my ear. 'Take yourself and your dusters elsewhere, Nelly.'

'I must do my work, miss,' I answered, at which she gave me a very sharp and painful nip in the arm.

'Oh, miss!' I cried. 'That's a nasty trick! You've no right to nip me and I won't put up with it!'

'I didn't touch you, you lying creature!' she said, blushing scarlet.

'What's that then?' I asked, showing the mark that was already turning purple.

She stamped her foot, and then, her wayward spirit getting the better of her, as it so often did, slapped me hard across the cheek.

'Catherine, love!' cried Linton, shocked at the behaviour of his idol.

Little Hareton, who had been quietly playing on the floor until now, set up a wailing, and babbled something about 'Wicked aunt Cathy'. That drew her fury down on to his own innocent head. She seized the child and shook him until he grew pale.

Linton sprang to take the child from her arms and handed him to me. For his pains, he received a stinging blow on his ear. He stepped back in astonishment, and then moved towards the door.

'That's right,' thought I. 'Take warning and be gone now that you have had a glimpse of what she's really like.'

'Where are you going?' demanded Cathy.

'I can't stay after you have struck me,' said Linton.

'Go, then,' said Cathy, 'and I'll cry – I'll cry myself sick!' And straight away she dropped to her knees by a chair, buried her face in its cushions and set to weeping. Linton took a step or two towards her.

'Miss is dreadfully wayward, sir,' I said. 'She's as bad as any spoiled child. You'd best be riding home, or she'll make herself sick just to annoy us and cause trouble.'

34

But the soft thing merely sat down, and reached out his hands to her. He had as much power to leave as a mouse caught by a cat. The two spent the rest of the afternoon together, murmuring into each other's ears. Then Hindley came home, fighting drunk, and ready to pull the house down around us. His return drove Linton speedily to his horse, and Cathy to her room.

I hid little Hareton, and took the shot out of the master's gun.

After Hindley had fallen asleep in the living room, I took Hareton from the kitchen cupboard, and sat with him on my knee, rocking him and singing softly, to soothe him. The poor child spent many a terrified hour in the darkness of that cupboard, listening to the raging of his father, and it always took a time to calm him down afterwards.

Later Heathcliff came in for his supper, and then left, so I supposed, to do his work in the stables. I was mistaken in this, as I discovered later. Because he knew that Hindley was insensible with drink, Heathcliff stayed in the kitchen, lying down on a settle that stood in a far dark corner.

It was then that Cathy crept into the room. 'Where's Heathcliff?' she asked.

'At his work with the horses,' I said. He didn't contradict me, or give away his hiding place; perhaps he had fallen into a doze and only woke later to hear what Cathy had to say.

'Oh, I'm so unhappy!' said she, sitting down on the hearth by my knee.

'A pity,' I replied. 'So many friends and so few cares, and yet can't be content!'

'Nelly, will you keep a secret for me?' she asked, gazing up at me in that way she had of making you love and forgive her, no matter what she had done before.

'Is it worth keeping?' I asked.

'Yes, it is. It worries me and I want to know what I should do. Edgar Linton has asked me to marry him and I've given him an answer. Before I tell you what it was, I want you to say what you think my answer ought to have been.'

'How can *I* say?' I told her. 'I think he is a fool to ask you, after seeing your behaviour this afternoon.'

She jumped to her feet at this. 'Well, he did and I accepted him. Say I did the right thing, Nelly!'

'Do you love him?' I asked.

'Of course I do!' she said. Then she sighed, and sat down at my knee once more. 'Nelly,' she said, 'do you ever have strange dreams? I dreamt that I was in heaven, and that it didn't seem like home, and I broke my heart with

weeping. The angels were so angry that they flung me back to earth, and I woke with joy to find myself in the middle of the moors. I have no more right to marry Edgar Linton than I have to be in heaven. If Hindley hadn't brought Heathcliff so low I should not have thought of it. But it would degrade me to marry Heathcliff now.'

It was then, sir, that I became aware of Heathcliff's presence. He stayed until he heard her say that it would degrade her to marry him, and then he rose in the shadows, and silently left the room.

CHAPTER 5

Cathy and Edgar

Little Hareton had fallen asleep, and I put him to bed and began to make our supper. Hindley still lay dead to the world in the other room, and would lie like that until morning. Joseph came in from the barn and sat at the table with clasped hands, waiting to give a blessing on the food. He did this at all our meals, and lengthy blessings they were too; many a plate of good hot food has gone cold while Joseph mumbled over it.

We were waiting for Heathcliff, and I went out to call to him, thinking that he was most likely in the barn. There was no answer. I returned to the kitchen and whispered to Cathy that I thought he might have heard what she had said about her possible marriage to Edgar Linton and how she thought that to marry Heathcliff would be degrading.

'Oh, what have I done?' she cried on hearing this, and began pacing the room. 'Oh, what can he have heard? Nelly, tell me, what did I say, I can't remember . . .'

'What a lot of mithering over nothing,' grumbled Joseph, and slapping his hat on his head, he went out to look for Heathcliff himself. He came back wet and more bad-tempered than ever.

'That lad gets worse,' he said. 'He's left the yard gate open and one of the ponies has trodden down two rigs of corn.'

'Did you find him, you old fool?' Cathy snapped.

'I'd be better off looking for the horse,' answered Joseph. 'As it is I can look for neither man nor beast on a night like this.'

It was a very dark night for summer, sir, and thunder was threatening. I suggested that we begin our meal, and that the rain would surely drive Heathcliff in. But Cathy was too upset to eat. She paced the kitchen floor, and then took to wandering down to the gate and back. At last she stayed by the road, and although I pleaded with her, nothing would persuade her to return to the warmth of the kitchen, even though the rain was beginning to fall in cold, heavy drops.

At midnight the storm broke over the Heights. There was a strong wind too. It brought down a tree which stood near the house and destroyed one of the chimney pots as it fell.

We thought a bolt had crashed into our midst and Joseph fell to his knees, pleading with the good Lord to spare the righteous – meaning himself, of course – and to strike only the ungodly, meaning the rest of us.

But the storm passed, and left all of us unharmed, except for Cathy. She came in as wet as she could be, and flung herself down on the settle, her face turned to the back.

'Well, miss,' I said, 'are you determined to get your death of cold? Come, let me rub your hair dry and then off to bed with you. Heathcliff will be in Gimmerton, and he'll probably stay the night.'

'No, no,' moaned that old misery, Joseph, 'he's more likely at the bottom of the bog. The bolt what brought down the tree were a sign from the Lord that we must mend our ways or go to everlasting damnation.'

So, having tried in vain to get Cathy to act sensibly, I left the two of them, one shivering and one preaching, and took myself to my own bed.

Nelly laid her knitting down in her lap at this point, and looked at me. 'And bed is where you should be, sir.'

'But your story takes my mind off my aches and pains so wonderfully, Nelly,' I told her in all truthfulness. 'It's much better than doctor's medicine.'

And so I coaxed her into going on with her tale.

◆◆◆

In the morning I came down to the kitchen, and threw open the window. How sweet everything smelled after the rain! But a moan from the settle made me turn, and there lay Cathy, pale and shivering.

Hindley chose this moment to enter the kitchen. 'What ails her?' he asked.

I saw that he was now sober and in his right mind, and he was a different person then.

'Oh, she is naughty!' I said. 'She got soaked in the storm last night, and I couldn't persuade her to go to bed.'

'She's ill,' said Hindley, laying his hand on her forehead. 'I suppose that's the reason she didn't go to bed. But what took you out, Cathy?'

'Running after lads, as usual,' croaked Joseph, who had also come in. 'Oh, never a day goes by when you're absent, master, but that Edgar Linton comes creeping to the house.'

He turned and nodded his head towards me.

'And her lets him in, and watches out for your return.'

'Be quiet!' said Cathy, rousing herself a little. 'Edgar called yesterday, Hindley, quite by chance, and I myself told him to go, as I knew you would not like him to be here . . . '

'Never mind Linton,' said Hindley. 'Were you with Heathcliff? I will not have you roaming the moors with that savage! If I find that you have been with him I shall turn him out of doors and he may fend for himself!'

'I didn't see Heathcliff last night,' said Cathy, beginning to sob bitterly. 'And if you do turn him out I'll go with him. But you may not have the chance. I may never see him again!'

'Put her to bed,' Hindley told me.

I half-carried her up the stairs, and I shall never forget the scene when we reached her room. It terrified me; I thought that she was going mad, and I begged Joseph to bring the doctor.

When he arrived he said that Cathy was delirious and dangerously ill. She had a fever and must be carefully nursed.

I am not a trained nurse, sir, but common sense came to my aid; I kept her as quiet as I could; and as she was strong, she began to mend. Edgar's mother, old Mrs Linton, paid us many a visit, and when Cathy was strong enough, insisted that she come to Thrushcross Grange to recover fully. The poor lady had reason to be sorry for her kind act; both she and her husband caught the fever and died within a few days of each other.

Cathy returned to us more passionate and haughty than ever. Heathcliff had never been heard of since the night of the storm, and one day, when Cathy had been particularly annoying, I turned on her and told her that she was the cause of his going. For several months after that she never spoke to me.

The doctor had told Hindley that she must not be crossed – that if she was refused anything that she wanted it could bring on a fit. And so Hindley gave in to her every whim. As for Edgar Linton, he believed himself to be the happiest man alive on the day he married Cathy in Gimmerton chapel.

Much against my will, I was persuaded to leave Wuthering Heights, and come to Thrushcross Grange. Little Hareton was now five years old, and I had just begun to teach him his letters. He cried bitterly when he learned that I was to leave him; but Cathy's tears were stronger. Edgar Linton offered me a magnificent wage; Hindley merely told me to pack my bag and leave.

So I kissed Hareton goodbye and since that day he has been a stranger to me. He no longer remembers Nelly Dean, and that he was once all the world to her.

I got Miss Cathy and myself to Thrushcross Grange, and I was surprised and a little disappointed to find that she behaved beautifully. I had braced myself to cope with her tantrums, as I had done at Wuthering Heights, and imagined that the rest of the household would admire me for my skill. But I did not get the chance to show off, for she was sweetness itself; indeed, she seemed to be a little *too* fond of Edgar Linton, as well as showing much love and affection for his sister, Isabella.

But I did notice that Edgar was frightened of putting her into a bad temper. Also, sir, she had days when she was very down. This was most unlike the old Cathy whose spirits had always been high, even at the worst of times. In those days she would overcome any unhappiness or sorrow or ill-treatment, but then, of course, she always had Heathcliff by her side. However, in spite of Cathy's dark moods and Edgar's fear of her temper, I thought that the two of them had a deep and growing happiness.

It ended. One soft evening in September, as I was coming from the garden with a basket of apples, I heard a voice behind me say, 'Nelly, is that you?'

It was a deep voice with a foreign tone, but there was something about the way it said my name.

Moving closer to the porch, I saw a tall man dressed in dark clothes and with a dark face and hair.

'You don't know me?' he said. 'I'm not a stranger. Look.'

He moved closer to the porch light, and I cried, 'What! Is it you?'

'Yes,' he said, 'it's Heathcliff. Where is she, Nelly? Go and tell her that a person from Gimmerton wishes to speak to her.'

'How will she take it?' I exclaimed. 'What will she do? The surprise bewilders *me* – it will turn Miss Cathy's head!'

'Do it!' he said roughly.

I couldn't say no to him, for I was afraid that if I did he would simply enter the house and find her for himself. I went to the parlour where Cathy and Edgar sat. 'A person from Gimmerton wishes to see you, ma'am,' I said.

'What does he want?' she asked.

'I didn't question him,' I told her.

She left the room, and Edgar enquired who the caller was.

'Someone the mistress doesn't expect,' I told him. 'It's Heathcliff – do you remember him, sir? He used to live at Wuthering Heights.'

'What! The gypsy! The ploughboy!' cried Edgar.

'Hush!' I told him. 'You mustn't call him by those names. She was heartbroken when he ran off.'

He went to the window and flung it open. 'Don't keep the visitor standing there, my love,' he called down to her. A moment later she burst into the room, and flung her arms round Edgar's neck.

'Oh, darling!' she cried. 'Heathcliff's back – he is!' and she hugged him harder than ever.

'Well, don't strangle me for it,' said Edgar. 'There's no need to be so frantic. He never struck *me* as being such a treasure.'

'I know you don't like him,' she answered, 'but for my sake you must be friends. Shall I tell him to come up?'

'Here?' said Edgar. 'In the parlour?'

'Oh, set a table for us in the kitchen, Nelly,' said my mistress. 'Heathcliff and I are too lowly for the gentlefolk in *this* room.' Her temper was flaring, I could see, and so could Edgar.

'Tell him to come up, Nelly,' he said, 'and Catherine, try to be glad without being ridiculous. The whole household needn't see you welcoming home a servant as though he were a brother.'

I went down to where Heathcliff waited on the porch, and led him to the parlour. He entered the room, and when I saw him clearly I was more amazed than ever at the change in him. He had grown into a tall, well-built man. Standing beside him, Edgar Linton looked slender, almost still a boy. My master's surprise was as great as mine, and he hardly knew how to behave towards someone whom he had thought of as a gypsy or a rough farmhand.

He sat a little apart from the two, who sat so close. I took my time in pouring their tea, and arranging little cakes and biscuits on a plate, and so was able to hear what was said.

'I heard of your marriage soon after I returned,' Heathcliff told Cathy. 'I meant to just have a glimpse of you, to return to Wuthering Heights, have my revenge on Hindley, and then leave at once before the law had its way with *me*.

'But when I saw you,' Heathcliff went on, 'that plan vanished entirely from my mind, and I now have another.'

I heard no more, for Edgar called to me, 'Nelly, you may go to the kitchen now,' and I left the room.

When the visit ended, I saw Heathcliff to the front door. 'You'll be staying in Gimmerton, I suppose,' I said.

'No, at Wuthering Heights,' he replied. 'Mr Earnshaw invited me when I called there this morning.'

I closed the door on him with feelings of amazement. Hindley invited *him,* and *he* called on Hindley!

'But now, sir,' said Nelly, with a firm tone to her voice, 'you must have some sleep.'

'I think, Nelly,' I said as she gathered up my supper things, 'that you are a true storyteller and like to leave your listener on the edge of his seat and eager for more.'

But she just smiled at this, and left the room.

CHAPTER 6

Heathcliff

All the next day, I thought about Heathcliff and Cathy, and wondered how it came about that Hareton, Hindley's own son, was now a lowly farmhand at Wuthering Heights. I wondered too how it was that the house now belonged to Heathcliff. When evening came I rang the bell for Nelly, my supper, and I hoped, the answer to these teasing questions.

Nelly took up her story at once.

◆◆◆

I was awakened in the night by Cathy coming to my room. 'I can't rest, Nelly,' she said. 'I must have another living creature near to share my happiness. Edgar is sulking because I praised Heathcliff and said how well he seems to have done!'

'What use is it to praise Heathcliff to him?' I asked. 'They didn't like each other as boys, so it's unlikely that they'll strike up a friendship now.'

'But it's so silly and childish to be jealous,' she said, curling up at the foot of my bed.

I couldn't resist asking her, 'What do you think of Heathcliff visiting Wuthering Heights?'

'Oh, he explained all that to me,' said Cathy. 'He called there just to get news of me, but found there was a card game in progress and joined it. It seems that he won a great deal of money from my brother, and Hindley asked him back. Heathcliff returned and won again. Then he offered to pay a high price to be allowed to lodge there. My brother, being what he is, agreed. So what he gets from Heathcliff in rent, he gives back to him in card games.'

'And he'll lose more than the rent of his rooms!' I thought to myself, understanding now in what way Heathcliff meant to get his revenge for all the childhood beatings he had suffered, and all his ill-treatment as a young man.

'You should be more careful of your husband's feelings,' I told Cathy. But she just laughed and said, 'I can't put up with such childishness!' and went her own way, as always.

So, Heathcliff visited Thrushcross Grange often, and he and Cathy were together in a private world of their own, just as they had been as children. Edgar Linton didn't like this, but was still afraid of crossing Cathy.

He wasn't alone in his unhappiness. We, that is the other servants and myself, had noticed that Miss Isabella was fretting and pining over something. The cause was supposed to be ill-health, for indeed she was fading before our eyes. But one morning over breakfast, she accused Cathy of treating her harshly.

'How have I been harsh?' asked Cathy. 'Tell me.'

'On our walk on the moor yesterday,' said Isabella, 'you told me to go where I pleased, while you went on with Mr Heathcliff.'

'And that's your idea of being harsh?' laughed Cathy. 'That wasn't because your company wasn't wanted, it was because I didn't think that anything Heathcliff might say would have any interest for you.'

'No,' wept Isabella, 'you wanted me to go away because you knew that I wanted to be there!'

'Is she sane?' asked Cathy, looking at me. Then she turned back to Isabella. 'I'll repeat our conversation word for word, and you can point out what charms it might have held for you.'

'It wasn't the conversation,' said Isabella. 'I wanted to be with him! And I won't always be sent away! You're a dog in the manger, Cathy, and desire no one to be loved but yourself.'

'I'll not believe this idiocy!' cried Cathy. 'Is it possible that you want Heathcliff to admire you – that you think him a good person? I hope that I've misunderstood you, Isabella.'

'No, you haven't!' said Isabella. 'I love him more than you love Edgar, and he would love me if only you'd let him.'

'Then I wouldn't be you for a kingdom,' said Cathy. 'Nelly, tell her what Heathcliff is: a fierce, pitiless, wolfish man. He'd crush you like a sparrow's egg, Isabella, if he found you troublesome. He couldn't love a Linton, I know, but he'd marry you for your money.'

Isabella ran from the room in tears. A little later I followed and found her weeping on her bed.

'Banish him from your thoughts, miss,' I told her. 'Cathy spoke strongly, but she knows him better than anyone. Ask yourself, how has he been living? How has he become rich? Why is he living at Wuthering Heights with a man he hates and has hated for years?'

She took no heed of my advice, nor did she mend her quarrel with Cathy. On the third day the master was called away on business, and as the two sat in icy silence, Heathcliff paid a call. I was brushing the hearth at the time, and saw the mischievous smile on Cathy's lips when she heard his name announced.

'Heathcliff!' she cried as he entered the room. 'Here are two people sadly in need of a third to thaw the ice between them; and you are the one whom we both would have chosen! Let me show you someone who loves you better than I do. My poor little sister-in-law is breaking her heart at the mere sight of your beauty.'

Isabella jumped up at this and would have left the room, but Cathy held her back, catching at her skirt and tugging it in a way that was meant to seem playful, but that I knew was not.

'We have been quarrelling like cats about you, Heathcliff,' said Cathy. 'And I have been told by my rival that if I had the good manners to stand aside, you would love her more than anything in the world!'

'Catherine! I said nothing of the kind!' cried Isabella.

Heathcliff remained silent and just stared at her, as though she was some strange repulsive insect. The poor thing couldn't bear that. After trying in vain to pull her skirt free, she ran her fingernails down the back of Cathy's hand.

'What a tigress!' said Cathy, letting Isabella go. 'How foolish to show those talons to *him*. Look, Heathcliff – beware of your eyes if she comes close.'

'I'd wrench them off her fingers if they ever threatened me,' he said.

With that they both seemed to dismiss the matter from their minds, but there had been something in Heathcliff's manner that made me decide to keep a close watch on him, and on Isabella too. His visits to the Grange were a nightmare to all, save Cathy, and I worried constantly about his living at Wuthering Heights. It seemed to me, sir, that God had forsaken that stray sheep, Hindley, to its own wicked and foolish ways, and that an evil beast prowled between it and the fold, waiting its time to spring and destroy.

CHAPTER 7

A Crisis

One day I became so worried about what might be happening at the farm, that I put on my bonnet and shawl and made my way to Wuthering Heights as fast as I could. There I found Hareton, *my* Hareton, gazing steadily at me through the bars of the gate.

'God bless you, darling!' I cried. 'It's Nelly, your old nurse!'

At once, he backed away and picked up a large flinty stone.

'I've come to see your father, Hareton,' I said,

disappointed that he did not know me, but telling myself that I had been away from him for ten months – a long time in the life of a small child.

Hareton raised his hand and threw his stone, at the same time uttering the most dreadful swear-words and oaths. This really upset me, sir, and I took an orange from my basket and held it out to him through the bars of the gate.

'Tell me who has taught you those fine words,' I said. 'Tell me and you shall have it.'

'Heathcliff!' came the answer. 'Heathcliff taught me.' A small brown hand shot out to grasp the fruit but I held it back.

'And do you like Heathcliff?' I asked.

'Oh, yes!' said Hareton. 'Better than anyone!'

I knew then that there was nothing I could do at Wuthering Heights to make things any better. I gave Hareton the orange and made my way back to the Grange.

Soon after this, Heathcliff came by when Isabella was feeding her pigeons in the courtyard. I saw them from the kitchen window. He went to her, said something that caused her to become flustered, and then drew her into his arms and kissed her.

'Traitor!' I exclaimed.

'Who is, Nelly?' asked Cathy, who had come into the kitchen without my knowing.

'Your worthless friend,' I told her. 'Ah, he's seen us and is coming in. I wonder if he'll have a good excuse for kissing Miss Isabella, when he has given every sign of hating her?'

He entered then, and Cathy turned on him. 'What do you mean by embracing Isabella?' she demanded.

'What is it to you?' he replied. 'I have a right to kiss her if she chooses, and you've no right to object.'

'Don't scowl at me,' said Cathy. 'If you like Isabella, then you shall marry her. Tell the truth, Heathcliff – do you love her? If you don't, then leave her be. You shan't play any games of revenge here!'

'I would as soon marry a monkey,' muttered Heathcliff – at which my mistress gave a cry of triumph.

'There!' she said. 'I knew it!'

'But I would do it,' he said, 'if it furthered my plans.'

I left the kitchen at this, and went in search of my master. I repeated to him what I had heard pass between Cathy and Heathcliff, and what I had seen pass between Heathcliff and Miss Isabella.

'This is disgraceful!' cried Linton. 'That she should insist in keeping such a brute as a friend! Call two men from the hall, Nelly. Catherine shall stay no longer with this fiend.'

He went down to the kitchen, and I and two manservants followed.

'I have put up with you for long enough,' my master told Heathcliff. 'In future stay away from my wife and from my sister. I give you three minutes to leave. After that, I shall throw you out!'

Heathcliff listened to this speech with both amusement and amazement.

'Cathy,' he said, 'this lamb of yours threatens like a bull. It is in danger of splitting its skull against my knuckles. Linton, I'm heartily sorry that you're not worth knocking down!'

My master signalled me to fetch the men who waited in the passage outside; he had no intention of tackling Heathcliff himself! But Cathy saw the signal, and guessed what was meant by it. As I turned to call, she pulled me back, slammed the door shut, and locked it.

'Play fair!' she said to Linton. 'If you haven't the courage to throw him out yourself, then apologize.'

Edgar made to take the door key from her, but she leapt back. 'No, I'll swallow it before you shall get it!' she said. 'I try to turn Isabella against Heathcliff by warning her of his true nature, and I force a confession from Heathcliff that he does not love Isabella. Edgar, I was defending you and yours, and this is how I am rewarded!'

Once more my master tried to take the key from her, and this time she flung it to the back of the fire. Edgar grew pale and trembled, and sank down into a chair, covering his face with his hands.

'Oh, this would have earned you a knighthood in the old days!' cried Cathy. 'Bear up, Edgar. Heathcliff would as soon lift a finger against you as a king would march an army against a mouse!'

'I wish you joy of the milk-blooded coward, Cathy,' said Heathcliff. 'And this is the shivering thing you preferred to me! Is he weeping, or is he going to faint from fear?'

He approached the chair where my master sat and gave it a push with his foot. It was not a wise move, for my master sprang up and struck him in the throat. It was a blow that would have felled a lesser man, and for a moment Heathcliff fought for breath. While he choked, Linton made his way through the back door, and out into the yard.

'There!' cried Cathy. 'Now you'll never be able to come here. Go now, for he'll be back with men and pistols!'

'Leave? With that blow burning in my gullet?' swore Heathcliff. 'No! I'll crush his ribs like a rotten hazelnut!'

'He's not coming,' said I, looking from the window. 'But two coachmen and the gardener are approaching, both with heavy clubs. Do you want to be thrown out of the house by the likes of *them*?'

Heathcliff took up the poker at this, smashed the lock on the door, and made his escape, as the men came into the kitchen.

Cathy was upset by all this, and asked me to accompany her to the living room. 'I am almost mad, Nelly,' she said. 'A thousand blacksmith's hammers are beating in my head. Tell Isabella to keep away from me; this is all her fault. And say to Edgar that I am in danger of becoming seriously ill. If Heathcliff must make horrid, vengeful plans, and if I can no longer have him for a friend on account of Edgar's jealousy, then I'll break both their hearts by breaking my own!'

She was quite capable of it, sir. From being a child, she had a will of iron.

My master came into the room just then, so I went into the next room, leaving the door ajar.

'I've come neither to make up our quarrel, Catherine, nor to go on with it,' he said. 'I have come for an answer. You must choose – is it to be Heathcliff or me? I need an answer.'

'And I need to be left alone,' said my mistress. She rang the bell until it broke, for I didn't hurry to her side; she was enough to try the patience of a saint with such senseless, wicked rages. She had thrown herself down on the sofa and there she lay, dashing her head against it and grinding her teeth. After a while she stretched out, as white and as stiff as though dead. My master stood gazing at her in fear.

'There is nothing in the world the matter,' I whispered to him.

'But she has blood on her lips,' he said with a shudder.

'Never mind,' I answered tartly, and I told him how she had deliberately planned to have this insane fit.

Foolishly, I spoke too loud and she heard me and darted up, her hair flying over her shoulders, her eyes flashing and the muscles of her neck standing out. I thought she would strike me, but she only glared at me and then rushed upstairs to her room.

My master told me to follow her. I did, but she had locked the door against me. The next morning the door was still locked and she refused breakfast. The same thing happened at tea and at dinner, and all through the following day.

My master kept to the library and didn't ask me about her. But he did see Isabella and made her promise that she would never speak to Heathcliff again. If the promise was broken, he said, he would no longer think of her as his sister.

CHAPTER 8

Cathy's Illness

For three days, Isabella moped in the garden, always in tears, and my master stayed in the library with books that he didn't read. He was very unhappy about Cathy, but pride wouldn't let him make the first move. I thought that he did the right thing, for she was far too fond of having her own way.

On the third day after Heathcliff's visit, she unbarred her door, and asked for some water. I took her some tea and dry toast, and she ate and drank eagerly. 'What is that unfeeling creature doing?' she asked, pushing her tangled hair away from her wasted face.

'If you mean Mr Linton,' I said, 'I think he's well. He spends a great deal of time with his books.'

'With his books!' she cried. 'And I am *dying*!' She couldn't bear the thought I had put into her head, that her husband sat happily reading. But I wouldn't have led her to believe that my master didn't care, had I known her true condition.

She tossed and turned feverishly and then tore at her pillow with her teeth. 'Open the window, Nelly,' she said, 'I am so hot.' We were in the middle of winter, sir, and a cold wind blew straight from the moors. I left the pane open for a few seconds, then closed it again. She seemed not to notice, but lay back, plucking feathers from the tear in her pillow. 'That's a turkey's,' she murmured to herself, 'that's a wild duck's; and this is a pigeon's.'

'Give over with that baby-work,' I said. 'Lie down and close your eyes.'

But I couldn't make her rest. 'Do you see that face?' she asked, staring at her own face in the mirror that hung on the wall.

'Why, it's you, Cathy,' I told her, but she just shuddered and cried that the room was haunted. I covered the glass with my shawl, now alarmed at the change that had come over her. I was about to leave the room to fetch my master when I was brought back by a shrieking cry. The shawl had slipped and she sat upright, staring at her face again.

I covered the mirror once more, and she lay back and became calmer. 'Oh, Nelly,' she said, 'I thought that I was in my old bedroom at Wuthering Heights. How I wish that I was there, with the sound of the wind in the trees. Do let me feel it. Do let me have one breath! Quick! Why don't you move?'

'Because I don't want to give you your death of cold,' I said.

'You won't give me a chance of life, you mean,' she said. 'I'm not helpless. I'll open it myself.'

She slid from the bed and walked very uncertainly to the window, threw it open and leant out. The frosty air blew in, cutting like a knife.

As I struggled to get her back into bed – her strength was much greater than mine, for she really *was* delirious – I heard the door-knob turn, and Mr Linton came into the room.

'Catherine!' he cried and tried to pull her away from the window. She turned on him in a fury.

'Oh, there you are!' she said. 'You are one of those

things that are there when least wanted, and when wanted – never!'

'What is she talking about?' asked my master, still struggling with Cathy.

'Her mind wanders, sir,' I told him. 'Just let's make her quiet and peaceful and she'll be all right.'

'I want no more advice from you, Nelly,' he replied. 'You knew what she was like, and yet you encouraged me to leave her alone. You didn't give me one hint of how she's been these last few days.'

Well, Mr Lockwood, I began to defend myself for I thought it wrong that I should be blamed for another's wicked ways. 'I know that Cathy is headstrong,' I cried, 'but I didn't know that you wished to give in to her fierce temper! I didn't know that I ought to have turned a blind eye to what went on between her and Heathcliff. Well, I'll know better next time. Next time you may find things out for yourself!'

Cathy had lain quiet in my master's arms during my speech, but now she began to struggle again. 'Traitor! Witch!' she screamed, and spat at me.

Leaving him to manage her as best he could, I set out to find Doctor Kenneth. As I hurried through the garden I caught a glimpse of Isabella's spaniel, Fanny, wandering round the shrubbery, and thought it strange that the little animal should be out alone at that time of night. I also thought that I heard the sound of a galloping horse. But there were more pressing things on my mind. I ran on, and was lucky enough to catch Kenneth leaving the house of a patient in the village.

As soon as he heard of Cathy's illness, he agreed at once to come back with me. While we made our way I told him what had happened, how the fit had been brought on by my master forbidding Heathcliff to visit the Grange, how my master had even struck him.

'I told Linton to be careful,' said Kenneth. 'I told him that she mustn't be crossed. This madness, Nelly, is the consequence. But I thought that he had become a friend to Heathcliff.'

'He put up with him for the sake of Cathy,' I told him. 'But then Heathcliff turned his attentions to Miss Isabella, and that caused the fight.'

'She's a sly one, is Isabella,' said Kenneth, 'but also a little fool. I have it from a reliable source that she and Heathcliff were walking in the Grange garden late last night and that he tried to persuade her to go with him there and then. He only left after she had promised to run away with him on their very next meeting.'

At this, I recalled the sight of the little spaniel wandering forlorn in the garden; I remembered too the distant sound of horse's hooves. Filled with foreboding, I ran ahead of Kenneth, and on reaching the Grange went straight to Isabella's room. It was empty.

I decided I shouldn't tell my master what had happened, as his mind was so filled with worry over Cathy. The news will keep until morning, I thought, for even if he had sent out servants to find the pair they would, by now, be far out of sight.

Kenneth arrived soon after. On examining Cathy he said that there was no danger of her dying, but that her brain might be damaged by the fever.

There was no sleep for either my master or myself that night.

In the morning I was spared the task of telling Edgar about Isabella. One of the maids, a thoughtless girl who had been on an early-morning errand to Gimmerton, came bursting in with the news.

'Oh, what next!' she cried. 'She's gone! Miss Isabella's gone. Gone off with Heathcliff! The blacksmith's lass saw them when they stopped to have a shoe fixed just after midnight.'

I ran to peep into Isabella's room, merely for form's sake, for of course I already knew it to be empty. 'Shall we send someone after them, sir?' I asked my master on my return.

He shook his head. 'She went of her own accord,' he said. 'Trouble me no more about her. From this time she is my sister in name only.' And that was all he said on the subject.

CHAPTER 9

Cathy's Child

Nothing was heard of Isabella and Heathcliff for two months. During that time Cathy was very ill with a brain fever. She recovered, but Doctor Kenneth had warned us that she would never be the same again. All her old spirit had gone and she lay pale and listless for weeks on end.

By now all the household knew that she was going to have a baby and we did our best to let her know how much we looked forward to the event. But nothing we said or did brought back the sparkle to her eye, or even a faint gleam of interest.

During this time I had a letter from Isabella. Her life at Wuthering Heights, she wrote, was dreadful. 'Is Heathcliff man or devil?' the letter asked. The news she gave me of Hindley was also bad. He drank and gambled and had lost the house to Heathcliff in a card game. Now he roamed about the place with a loaded pistol in his pocket, waiting, he said, for a chance to shoot his tormentor. 'Although,' wrote Isabella, 'I doubt that he will ever find the courage to do so.'

In this she was right. The next news I had from the Heights was of the death of Hindley, who died without recovering even a small part of his rightful inheritance.

Then word reached me that Isabella had run away; but where she went, I never discovered.

Of Heathcliff I heard nothing, but often thought that I saw him late at night, standing amongst the trees in the parkland of the Grange, watching Cathy's window. I dismissed this as fancy on my part. But on the night that little Catherine was born something drew him closer to the house, and I saw him clear enough. He looked frightful, as though he had not slept in days. Despite his wicked ways I felt sorry for him, and went out to him as soon as I could.

'Tell me, Nelly,' he said, 'what has happened?'

'The child is born,' I told him, 'but Cathy is dead.'

My master scarcely left his room after the death of Cathy, and I took over the care of little Catherine, just as I had taken care of Hareton. The next twelve years were the happiest of my life. She was the most winning thing that ever brought sunshine to a desolate house, mild and gentle as a dove, and with none of her mother's wild ways about her. Until she was thirteen she had not gone beyond the parkland that surrounded the Grange. She had no idea that Wuthering Heights and Heathcliff existed, but she longed to explore the moors, and constantly asked me for stories about the places where her mother had played as a child, places such as Penistone Crags and the fairy cave.

Then, one day, she was nowhere to be found.

I wandered the grounds asking all I met if they had seen her. At last I got my answer.

'Why, she leapt her pony over the hedge and galloped away,' said a labourer who was mending a fence. He might, I thought, have been talking about Cathy, my dead mistress.

'The little minx!' thought I, then fell to wondering if perhaps her mother's nature was coming out in her after all. I made my way as fast as I could along the path which led over the moors, but there was no sign of her, although I looked about me constantly as I went.

At last I reached Wuthering Heights. 'You'll be looking for your little mistress,' said the servant who let me in. 'She's here, safe and sound! But thank goodness that the master wasn't at home!'

And there she was, sitting contentedly in a little rocking chair which had belonged to her mother.

'Well, miss!' I said. 'This is your last ride until your father returns.' He was away on business but was expected back the next day. 'To go stealing off like this! It shows what a cunning little fox you are!'

This caused the tears to flow, for I was rarely strict with her; indeed, I scarcely had reason ever to speak to her harshly.

'Don't be hard on her,' said the servant. 'She was going to ride back straight away, but I thought it best that Hareton went with her, and she was waiting for him to come from the fields.'

Hareton, during all this, stood with his hands in his pockets, too awkward to speak.

I took Catherine's hat from its hook on the wall. 'Come, miss,' I said, 'let's be on our way.'

But to spite me for my hard words perhaps, she darted away from me. The servant and Hareton laughed. Feeling foolish, I snatched at her arm, and made her stand still.

'Well, Miss Catherine,' I told her, 'if you knew whose house this is, you would be glad to get away!'

'It's your father's, isn't it?' asked Catherine, turning to Hareton.

Hareton blushed scarlet and mumbled, 'No.'

'Oh, you must be a servant,' said Catherine. 'Very well, then, fetch my horse.'

She turned back to me. 'I suppose that you're right and we should leave.' Then seeing that Hareton made no move, she said, 'Well, go! What are you waiting for?'

'I'll see you damned before *I'll* be your servant!' said Hareton.

'You'll see me *what*?' asked Catherine in surprise.

'Damned, you saucy witch!' said Hareton.

'Nelly!' cried Catherine. 'How dare he speak to me like that! He must be made to do what I say or I'll tell Papa!'

Hareton did not appear to be much bothered by this threat.

'You bring my pony then!' she said, turning to the woman.

'Softly, miss,' said the servant, 'you'll lose nothing by being polite. And although Hareton here may not be the master's son, he is kin to you – he's your cousin.'

'He's not! He's not!' cried Catherine, flinging herself into my arms and eager enough now to leave the house.

We made our way home, sadly out of sorts. But I couldn't get any details out of my little lady of how she had spent the day. She had managed to reach Penistone Crags, and from there she made her way to Wuthering Heights, where she met Hareton. He showed her the fairy cave, and other places, and it seemed she had very much liked him until the time when she took him for a servant and he called her 'witch' – she who had always been 'darling' and 'queen' and 'angel' to all around her, to be so shockingly insulted by a stranger! It was all I could do to persuade her not to tell her father about it.

'If he ever finds out I let you go to that house,' I told her, 'I shall have to leave.'

Catherine couldn't bear the thought, and promised never to tell. She would keep her word, I knew, for after all, she was a sweet little girl.

CHAPTER 10

Linton Comes Home

Soon after Catherine's visit to Wuthering Heights a letter arrived for my master. It was to tell him that Isabella was dead. But she left a son, and straight away Edgar set out to bring the boy to the Grange. Catherine ran wild with joy at the thought that she would have a playmate. True, she amused herself well enough, but I had often thought it a pity that she was an only child.

On the day of Linton's arrival – Isabella had named him after her brother – Catherine went down to the main gate a dozen or more times, and at last ran back to the kitchen, crying, 'They're here! They're here!'

Oh, sir, he looked so like Edgar that he might almost have been his young brother – he had the same pale, delicate air; but there was also a peevishness about him that was never found in his uncle.

'Now, Catherine,' said her father, 'your little cousin isn't as strong as you, and you must take care not to tire him.'

'Oh, I will, Papa!' she said. 'I wouldn't do anything to make him unhappy.'

'There now, Linton,' said my master. 'Your cousin is fond of you already. You have nothing to do now but rest and amuse yourself.'

'Let me go to bed then,' said the boy, and off he trailed in the care of a servant. Catherine went with him to sit by his side until he slept.

'I think he'll do very well, Nelly,' said my master, 'once he has the company of another child. If we keep him, Catherine will put new spirit in him.'

'Yes, if we *can* keep him!' thought I.

Late that night the maid told me that Heathcliff's servant, Joseph, wished to see the master.

'What is it, Joseph?' I asked, going down to the kitchen to speak with him. 'Mr Linton's gone to bed. He's tired out with travelling.'

'Heathcliff has sent me for his lad,' said Joseph. 'I mustn't go back without him.'

I went upstairs to waken my master; Joseph followed me, barging into the bedroom and stating at once the reason for his visit.

'He wants his lad!' he said.

My master didn't seem surprised by the request. 'Tell Mr Heathcliff that his son shall come to Wuthering Heights tomorrow,' he said, speaking calmly but with an expression of great sorrow. 'You may also tell him that the child's mother wanted him to stay with me. His health is not good.'

'No!' said Joseph. 'That means nothing. Heathcliff must have his lad, and I must take him now!'

My master rose from his bed at this, and grasping Joseph by the elbow, thrust him from the room. 'Go back and tell your master what I have said. The boy will be sent to him in the morning.'

'Very well!' shouted Joseph, as he made his way back down the stairs. 'Tomorrow he'll come himself. Thrust *him* out if you dare!'

So that this threat could not be carried out, my master told me to take Linton to Wuthering Heights at the crack of dawn. And I was on no account to tell Catherine where he had gone.

Linton was very cross at being woken at five the next morning. 'Where are we going?' he asked fretfully.

'Why, you are going to see your father, Linton!' I said, trying to make the whole thing sound like a merry jaunt, just a visit that would come to an end as visits almost always do.

But the child shrank back, and stared at me. 'My *father*?' he whimpered. 'But I don't have a father.'

'He lives in a big house, over the moor,' I said, ignoring his distress, 'and you must learn to love him, and then he will love you.'

We set out then, Linton on Miss Catherine's pony,

and myself on the old pony, Minnie. I thought about the lies I had told the poor child and did my best to soften them, or at least bring them a little nearer to the truth.

'He may not be so gentle and kind at first,' I said, 'but he will come to love you better than any uncle, for you are his very own.'

We reached Wuthering Heights and found Heathcliff, Joseph and Hareton at breakfast.

'Bring it in then, Nelly,' said Heathcliff, as Linton stood shivering on the doorstep. I gently urged him forward until he stood in the glow of the light.

The three men stared at him; then Joseph broke into his cackling laugh.

'Eh, I think Edgar Linton's swopped you, master, and that's his lass!'

'My, what a beauty!' said Heathcliff. 'What did they rear it on?'

'I hope that you're going to be kind to the boy, Mr Heathcliff,' I said. 'Remember, he's all the kin you have in the world.'

'Oh, I'll be kind, Nelly,' said he. 'I wish to see my son become owner of Thrushcross Grange. I cannot let him die until he has it. Then I shall inherit it from him. For that reason, I will put up with him, though I can barely stand the sight of the weak little thing.'

I was mystified, but I had no excuse to stay longer. I slipped out while poor Linton was timidly backing away from a friendly sheep dog.

'Don't leave me here!' I heard him shout. 'I'll not stay here!' But the door was firmly closed and I heard the key turn in the lock.

I mounted the pony, and leading Miss Catherine's pony, rode home. There was nothing else that I could do.

CHAPTER II

A Trap is Set

We had a sad time with little Catherine that day. She rose full of eagerness to see her cousin, and couldn't understand why he had left so soon. I have no idea what her father told her, but he promised that Linton would return.

For a long time, every morning she asked me, 'Is Linton coming back today?' Then little by little his memory faded, and she quite forgot him. But I couldn't forget the sight of that pale face, and the fear in the blue eyes when the child had been given to his father. True, in the small time that I'd known him I'd found him spoiled and fretful, but no doubt Isabella had coddled him, and so it was scarcely the child's fault that he was as he was.

Sometimes I heard news of him when I met up with one of the servants at the Heights; but it was never good.

'I never knew such a fearful, weakly child,' she told me. 'He's forever ailing, forever sitting by the fire wrapped in his fur cloak. And if Hareton, who's not a bad lad despite his rough and ready ways, tries to amuse him it always ends in tears. As for the master, he can't stand the child.'

I heard versions of this tale many times over the years. But I never met him again, and neither did Catherine – her father kept her confined to the parklands of the Grange – until the day of her sixteenth birthday.

We never celebrated the event as it was also the day that her mother had died. But on that particular birthday she came to me, full of excitement. While riding out with her father she had seen where the grouse had flown and she dearly wanted to go back to see the eggs. Her father was away from home on that day and, to my regret, I let her talk me into going with her.

How easily I was fooled! We rode until we were almost at the high crags at Penistone. 'Where are your birds, Miss Catherine?' I said. 'We're a long way from the Grange now, you know.' I was beginning to suspect that there were no birds and that the little minx had merely wanted to explore.

'Not much farther, Nelly!' she cried, and rode off at a canter leaving me well behind on the stout old pony, Minnie.

She stopped some distance away and before I could catch up with her, two people appeared at her side. At once I knew them to be Heathcliff and Hareton. When I reached her, she was protesting that all she had wanted to do was see the birds' eggs. Heathcliff, I must tell you, sir, owned all the shooting rights to the land, and wouldn't put up with poachers. Not that I thought for one moment he imagined Catherine to be a stealer of birds and their eggs. No, it was just an excuse to keep her talking. I knew his ways, and he knew that *I* knew, for he glanced at me and gave a wry smile.

'Well, now that I know you're not after my birds,' he said, 'I would be honoured if you and your nurse would come to my house and take tea with me. It is quite near and I should like you to meet my son.'

'This is not your son?' asked Catherine, turning her gaze on Hareton.

'I'm not his son,' muttered Hareton, blushing scarlet.

'Miss Catherine,' I whispered urgently in her ear, 'you must *not* accept this invitation.'

But Heathcliff brushed me aside. 'Hareton,' he said, 'go on ahead with our guest, and Nurse and I will follow.'

When they were out of earshot he told me what he planned. 'I hope that she and Linton will fall in love and marry. That way, Nelly, I gain both Wuthering Heights *and* Thrushcross Grange. My son is in poor health, and his will leaves everything to me. I have made sure of that.'

We had reached the gates of Wuthering Heights by this time, and there was no turning back. 'Well, you've tricked us this time,' I said, 'but I shall make sure that she never comes here again!'

Once inside the house, Heathcliff pointed to Linton

and said, 'This is my son, Miss Catherine, and you two have met before. This is Linton.'

'Why, Linton!' cried Catherine, running forward and kissing him.

'Catherine!' he said, and I saw from his delight in seeing her again that Heathcliff's plan had every chance of succeeding.

As soon as my master returned, I told him what had happened. He took Catherine to his study and told her that she must never see Linton again. If he gave her any reasons for this, I never discovered them, for she refused to speak to me for days.

But apart from this, she soon grew more like her old self once more, riding about the grounds of the Grange on her pony for hours at a time. I relaxed my watch, sir. No one from the Heights came near the place, and I supposed that Linton had given up all thoughts of ever seeing her again.

But I was wrong, for soon after, I found the little bundle of letters that she had hidden in her drawer. How did she get them, and how did she send her replies? I took up my watch again, and soon discovered that a kitchen hand acted as postman. I then sent my own note: 'Master Heathcliff is not to send any more notes to Miss Catherine, as she will neither read them, nor reply to them.'

After that, I told her there would be no more letters.

Summer came to an end, and all seemed well at Thrushcross Grange until my master fell ill. Nothing that Doctor Kenneth or I could do seemed to make him any better. Catherine became more and more worried. She grew thinner and paler. One brisk autumn day, when her father did seem a little easier and slept, under the watchful eye of a good nurse, I persuaded her to take a walk with me over the moors.

The exercise seemed to do her good, and I was glad I had made the suggestion, until the sky suddenly grew darker and a rainstorm threatened. At the same time I saw Heathcliff making his way towards us, mounted on his roan horse. How fitting, I thought, that these two dark events should occur together!

'Come, Miss Catherine,' I said, 'we must get back before it begins to rain.'

But Heathcliff had already reached us. 'Well, Miss Linton!' he said. 'Would you care to know how my son is, since you were so wicked as to break his heart?'

'Don't listen to him, miss,' I said. 'If anyone is wicked, it is himself!'

But her gentle heart was touched, and as usual, she got her own way. The next evening saw me riding by her side, on our way to Wuthering Heights.

The weather was still very damp and cold, and we reached the house to find scarcely any fire in the grate.

Linton was huddled in an armchair, wrapped in a thick cloak. His face was pale as milk, and there were dark rings under his eyes. I hurried to stir the fire a little, but he complained that I was making the ashes fly into the air, and he began to cough. Catherine crouched by his side, and took hold of his thin hand. She was close to tears, I knew.

'Miss,' I said, 'this is none of your doing. He was always sickly as a child.'

'It *is* of her doing,' said Linton. 'At least, she has made me worse.'

'How?' I asked.

'She didn't come to see me,' he replied, 'and she was the only nice, good person I knew. They all hate me here.'

There was truth in what he said, I had to admit, and I felt a great deal of sympathy for him. But my main concern was for my young mistress. The place was icy cold, and call though I might, no servant came to bring more coal for the fire.

'They don't come,' said Linton, 'no matter how much I call.'

We stayed an hour or more, Catherine running all kinds of little errands for him. Neither would accept *my* services; Catherine would do his bidding and he would have only her attend him. And so it was, sir, sitting unmoving in that cold room I took a bad chill. When we returned to

Thrushcross Grange, I took to my bed and stayed there for three weeks with a fever and aching bones.

This was my little lady's chance, and as I later learned from one of the servants, she rode out to meet Linton nearly every day.

CHAPTER 12

Treachery

I heard the story of Catherine and Linton over several evenings, then Nelly asked for a few days off to visit her sister. I could hardly refuse to let her go, but the evenings were very dull without the sound of her soft country voice, and the click of her knitting needles.

And then one morning, gazing out over the moors in the direction of Wuthering Heights, the question came to me, like a clap of thunder: could the beautiful girl I met at the house be the Catherine Linton of Nelly's story?

I asked Betsy, the young servant who had taken over Nelly's duties, if she knew if this was so, but she merely said, 'Couldn't say, I'm sure, sir.'

But I felt certain that my guess was right, and on the evening of Nelly's return I learned that I was indeed correct.

'Catherine Linton that was,' she said, 'Catherine Heathcliff as she is now.'

'What!' I exclaimed. 'She married that brute of a man! Why, he's old enough to be her father'

'No, sir, no,' interrupted Nelly, 'she married Heathcliff's son – Linton.'

To my great satisfaction, the story then continued.

When I learned of her meetings with Linton, my first thought was to tell her father. But then I thought again, sir. My master was still very weak and kept mostly to his room. What good would it do him to learn of Catherine's behaviour? And I thought of Catherine, too; she had no one at all for a companion, and it was small wonder that she had seized whatever chance she could of a little friendship and fun.

At first I tried to make her promise me that the meetings would now end, but she begged so hard that they might continue that I soon gave in. Linton was so often ill, she said, and her visits were his only pleasure. This I could well believe, with a father like Heathcliff! And so, a few mornings later found us both trotting our ponies over the moors to where I saw Linton waiting in the distance. As we drew near, another figure appeared. It was Heathcliff.

'Why, miss,' I said, 'you never told me that he too was present at your meetings.'

'Why Nelly,' she replied, 'he never was before!' I knew

from the surprised tone of her voice that she spoke the truth.

'Well, Miss Linton,' said Heathcliff, 'I think that today, instead of keeping yourselves to the moors, you and my son – and you too, Nelly Dean – should pay a more civilized call and take tea at my house.'

I glanced at Linton and saw that he was deathly pale and that he trembled. 'Please, Catherine,' he whispered, 'do as he says.'

'No, miss!' I said, leaning from my saddle and reaching for the bridle of her pony, to turn its head homewards. 'You mustn't. It will be some sort of trick!'

But her thoughts were only of Linton.

'What harm can there be, Nelly?' she said.

Heathcliff echoed her words. 'What harm? My house is not stricken with the plague.'

And so we rode on to Wuthering Heights, where he ushered us in, closed the door – and locked it.

Catherine stood a moment, hardly believing what had happened, then she flew at him, and tried to seize the key.

'Stop that,' he said, 'or I shall knock you down!'

She ignored the warning, tried to prize open his fingers, and finally bit his hand; at which he struck her several times on the side of her head.

I ran to her side and tried to pull him off, but a push in the chest sent me reeling back. Being stout, I am easily put out of breath.

'Now go to Linton,' he said to Catherine. But she came to me, and buried her face in my lap.

Heathcliff, cool as a cucumber, made the tea. (None of his servants were in the house, an arrangement made no doubt to fit in with his plan.)

'I will now go and see to your horses,' he said, and left, for all the world the perfect host – except that the key was again turned in the lock.

Catherine then turned on Linton. 'You *knew* that this

was what he planned!' she said. She was angry now, rather than afraid.

'Please, Catherine,' whimpered Linton. 'I couldn't help it. He said he'd kill me if I didn't do as he asked.'

'And what did he ask?' she demanded.

'He wants us to get married,' said Linton. 'He's afraid of my dying if we wait, and so we're to marry in the morning. Then when I die, and your father dies, Thrushcross Grange will be his.'

'You little monster!' I cried. 'No one would be sorry if you *did* die, I'm sure.'

'And my father isn't going to die!' said Catherine, and she looked to me for reassurance. 'He's *not*, is he, Nelly?'

'Indeed no!' I told her. 'He's still weak, but he gains strength every day.' My lie convinced her that all would be well.

Soon after this, Heathcliff returned with one of the servants and we were shown a room where we were to spend the night. Once again, a key was turned on us. Catherine sat by the window and gazed out, waiting and hoping for someone from the Grange to come to enquire after us. But when, after some hours, two servants rode up, we found that the window could not be opened. We hammered with our fists, but were too far away for our summons to be heard, and the servants rode away.

In the morning, Heathcliff knocked on the door and asked if Catherine were awake – as if we could have slept, worrying what torments my poor master must be going through. When she ran to open the door, he snatched her out, thrust me back, and locked the door again.

And there I remained, sir, for five days and nights.

CHAPTER 13

— ◄◆► —

Heathcliff's Revenge

On the sixth morning, after my breakfast had been brought, the door to the room was left unlocked. I waited, as I had waited every morning, for the sound of the key turning in the lock. It didn't come, and hurrying down the stairs, I found the front door also open, and the living room filled with sunlight.

Linton lay on the settle. 'Where's Miss Catherine?' I demanded. 'Has she gone?'

'Oh, no,' he answered, 'she can't go. We won't let her. She's my wife now, and must do everything I say.'

'Where *is* she?' I repeated.

'Locked in her room,' said Linton. 'But you shan't have the key. No one knows where it is but Father and me.'

'And where is your father?'

'In the courtyard, talking to Doctor Kenneth. He says that Catherine's father is dying. When he does, Thrushcross Grange will be mine, won't it.'

I could bear neither the sight nor the sound of the spoiled, selfish thing for a moment longer. I ran from the room and made my way over the moors as quickly as I could.

The servants at the Grange, who had thought both Miss Catherine and I dead in some bog, greeted me with astonishment and joy. I assured them that she was well, and would follow shortly; then I hurried up the stairs to tell the news to my master.

What a change I found in him! I feared that what Doctor Kenneth had said was right. 'She'll soon be here, sir,' I murmured, bending over him, and I saw him stir a little. 'Catherine is safe and well, and will come home soon.'

Then I sent a manservant to hire a lawyer, and to find and bring my little mistress home. He returned to say that Heathcliff had told the lawyer that Catherine was ill, but that she would return to us as soon as she was well.

Fools! I thought, not to see through this trick. I gathered together four of our strongest men, and armed them with my master's guns, determined to find Catherine.

But I was spared the task, for just as we were about to set out, the door was flung open and in she rushed.

Her hair was wild, her dress torn, her hands cut and bleeding. She had been locked in the same room that had once imprisoned her mother – and just as her mother had done, she had escaped through the window. From there she had made her way down to the ground by a low sloping roof and the branches of a tree.

'Nelly!' she cried. 'He's not dead, is he?'

'No, miss,' I said, 'but there is not much time left.'

She was with him when he died.

Soon after the funeral of my master, Heathcliff paid a visit to the Grange. His purpose, he stated, was to take Catherine back to Wuthering Heights. 'Your husband needs you,' he told her. 'He is ill. Your place is by his side. The law says so, miss. Hurry and pack your things!'

She didn't even try to argue with him, knowing it to be useless, but just went to her room, and returned in a short while with a bag. 'Nelly,' she said, 'is my pony saddled?'

'You may do without your pony,' said Heathcliff. 'It's a fine night, and we'll walk. You'll need no ponies at

Wuthering Heights. The only journeys you'll make there,
your own feet will take you.'

She bent and kissed my cheek, and that was the last I
saw of my little mistress.

'And that, sir,' said Nelly, 'is the end of my story.'

CHAPTER 14

Return to Wuthering Heights

Soon after this I left the Grange and travelled about Europe. I was away from England for some two years. On my return, I went to shoot grouse at the manor of a friend of mine. I had never stayed with this friend before and was surprised to see, on my journey there, a signpost with the name 'Gimmerton'. I had not realized that I was so near my old home.

I couldn't of course resist making my way as soon as I could, to see my dear servant, Nelly Dean. But at Thrushcross Grange I was told that she now lived at Wuthering Heights.

'She works for *that* man?' I exclaimed. 'That villain Heathcliff?'

'Nay, sir,' said the girl who had opened the door to me. 'Heathcliff's dead!' She gazed at me for a moment, then added, 'There was something odd about it, sir. Everyone says so.'

I hurried straight to the Heights and found Nelly sitting on a wooden bench under the window of the house. She was shelling peas into a bowl held in her lap, and as she worked she glanced fondly at Catherine who sat close by in the little garden. Hareton sat at Catherine's side, and their two heads were bent over a book.

I approached softly, not wanting to disturb this peaceful scene, but Nelly heard the creak of the gate and jumped to her feet, only narrowly saving the peas from being scattered over the path.

'Why, Mr Lockwood, sir!' she exclaimed.

'Nelly!' I replied, going up to her, and nodding towards the young pair in the garden. The house itself seemed brighter, sunnier, with its doors open to the air, and with fresh curtains at its windows. 'What a change! And how come you to be *here* of all places?'

◆◆◆

Sir, two months after Heathcliff took Catherine from the Grange he sent for me. And right glad I was to go, and was welcomed by my mistress with tears and open arms! Linton was ill, and lay all but lifeless on the settle. He didn't move from it day or night, so Zillah told me, but just moaned and fretted. Doctor Kenneth said there was little to be done, and, she said, it was certain that neither Heathcliff nor Catherine did anything to make him easier. He died and was buried with little grieving on the part of either Catherine or his father.

In fact, sir, the one who seemed sorriest for the poor creature's death was Hareton. I think he regarded Linton as sick weakly animal, to be looked after as best as was possible. Of course, Heathcliff continued to treat Hareton himself as a farmhand.

As for Catherine, Heathcliff couldn't bear the sight of her.

I don't blame Catherine for her treatment of Linton. She had truly loved him and he repaid her love with treachery. As for Heathcliff, I supposed that his guilty conscience troubled him each time he looked at her. Little wonder my poor young mistress kept to her room.

But she had one friend, even though she was rude to him at first. Hareton began showing his concern for her by laying books at her door; books that he was using to try to teach himself to read. In my first few days at the Heights I heard him stumbling over the simplest words. But that old misery Joseph cackled away to himself about how it was 'late in the day for any learning,' and how he had best keep to his place in life, the place where the good Lord had seen fit to put him.

This roused Hareton, who by rights ought to have been the owner of Wuthering Heights. Catherine took his side; she too had been cheated out of her inheritance. She began to teach Hareton to read, and a right quick scholar he proved to be.

She had steeled herself to stand up against Heathcliff over these lessons. I too imagined the books would be flung to the back of the fire; but nothing of the sort took place. A change had come over Heathcliff, and he seemed not to notice what went on around him.

I asked if he were ill, but he just shook his head. He moved from his bedroom to a smaller room, and night after night we heard the sound of his footsteps as he

paced back and forth, back and forth. Then one night, when I carried up some candles for him, I found him leaning out through the open casement window. It seemed to me as though he had been talking, or calling to someone below, but when I set the candles on the little shelf and glanced down there was no one to be seen.

I thought that the whole thing had been my fancy, sir, but night after night we heard him call, heard the creak of the casement window as it was blown back and forth – for sometimes, he fell into a doze and slept for a time with his head on the window ledge and the wind blowing the pane to and fro.

◆◆◆

'Nelly!' I said. 'He was in the room where I was lodged. The room with the little cabinet and the names "Catherine Earnshaw", "Catherine Heathcliff" and "Catherine Linton".'

'You know then, sir,' said she, and gave me a keen glance.

'It was the worst night of my life, Nelly,' and I told her about the spirit that had called to me. 'It seemed like a bad dream,' I said, 'but it was real. It was very real.'

'I don't doubt it, Mr Lockwood,' she replied. 'I think that at last she came for Heathcliff. Cathy came. I heard his footsteps on the stairs, and the slam of the door as he left the house. It was in the small hours of the morning, and he didn't return. He was found dead, close by where Cathy is buried, and is now buried there himself.

'In his will he gave the two houses back to their rightful owners: Wuthering Heights to Hareton and Thrushcross Grange to Catherine.'

She rose from the bench, holding the bowl. 'Come into the house and have some tea, sir,' she said.

'And so that is the end of the story,' I remarked, following her, with a backward glance at the young couple in the garden. They were laughing and gazing lovingly at each other. 'And a happy ending too!'

'Not quite the end, sir,' said Nelly, after she had rung for the tea to be brought. 'I was walking on the moor some time after Heathcliff died, and came across a little shepherd lad. He was in tears. "Have your lambs strayed, my bonny?" I asked. "Shall I help you look for them?"

' "My lambs are safe," said the lad. "It's Heathcliff. Heathcliff and a woman are up there, and I daren't go past!"

'I thought at first that this was just a child's fancy, but others have seen them, sir, seen the two of them together. They say that their ghosts haunt the moors.'

I stayed with Nelly for some time longer, and then made my way back on foot. When I reached the two graves I paused for a time, gazing at Cathy's headstone, now covered with moss, and at Heathcliff's which was raw, bare stone. It was a gentle night, dusk was falling and moths fluttered amongst the heath and the harebells. As I listened to the soft wind breathing through the grass, I wondered how anyone could ever imagine anything but peace for the sleepers in that quiet earth.

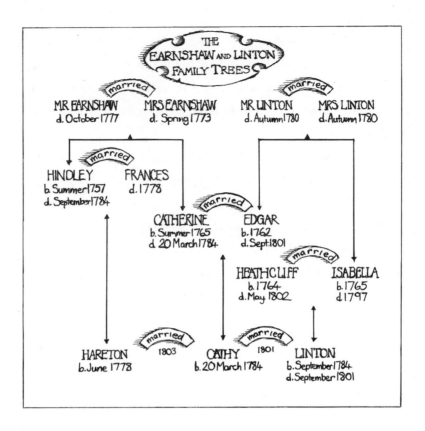

THE
EARNSHAW AND LINTON
FAMILY TREES

married

MR EARNSHAW   MRS EARNSHAW   MR LINTON   MRS LINTON
d. October 1777   d. Spring 1773   d. Autumn 1780   d. Autumn 1780

married

HINDLEY   FRANCES
b. Summer 1757   d. 1778
d. September 1784

married

CATHERINE   EDGAR
b. Summer 1765   b. 1762
d. 20 March 1784   d. Sept. 1801

married

HEATHCLIFF   ISABELLA
b. 1764   b. 1765
d. May 1802   d. 1797

married   *married*
HARETON   1803   CATHY   1801   LINTON
b. June 1778   b. 20 March 1784   b. September 1784
                                            d. September 1801

104